BOBS AND Tweets
The New Dog in Town

CHOPPER

by PEPPER SPRINGFIELD

illustrated by KRISTY CALDWELL

SCHOLASTIC INC.

For Emily, a true dog lover.
–PS

For Alexis
–KC

All rights reserved. Published by Scholastic Inc., *Publishers since 1920*. SCHOLASTIC and associated logos are trademarks and/or registered trademarks of Scholastic Inc.

The publisher does not have any control over and does not assume any responsibility for author or third-party websites or their content.

ISBN 978-1-338-64530-9

10 9 8 7 6 5 4 3 2   21 22 23 24

Printed in the U.S.A.   40
First edition, November 2020

Book design: Becky James
Color Flatter: Mike Freiheit

TABLE OF CONTENTS

CHAPTER 1
SPECIAL DELIVERY

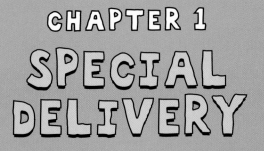

Bob Four is asleep. Chopper barks at the door.

Bob Four groans, "Stop barking! I want to snooze more."

He looks out the window. "Nobody there."

He goes back to sleep in his big napping chair.

Dean Bob plays chess with his best friend, Lou Tweet.

He hears Chopper barking across Bonefish Street.

"I need to feed Chopper. It is time that he ate."

"No problem-o," says Lou. "But I win: Checkmate."

Six Tweets rake leaves in their front yard.

"Dean, look," Tweet Four points. "A gift with a card.

A special delivery came around two."

"It looks like a fruit basket. Who sent it?" asks Lou.

Dean looks both ways. He crosses the street.

A fruit basket? he thinks. *That would be sweet.*

He reads the large note: "Please! Take care of Jack."

Dean peeks in the basket. He yells and jumps back!

CHAPTER 2
JACK

The Tweets run fast when they hear Dean Bob scream.
Bob Four sighs, "You woke me from such a nice dream."
"Look at him!" Lou coos. "A cute little pup."
Chopper growls. Dean scolds, "Chopper, please give it up!"

Dean and Lou get down on their hands and their knees.
"Watch out!" Tweet Four warns. "That dog might have fleas."
"Is Jack ill?" Lou wonders. "He looks pretty sad."
"Abandoned!" Dean groans. "This makes me *so* mad."

Bob Four cuddles Jack. They sit down to discuss.
Dean asks, "Why would Jack's family send him to us?"
"Perhaps," Tweet Four peeps, "this dog has rabies.
I bet he went mad and bit a few babies."

"Or zombies attacked Jack's house," cries Bob Four.

"His owners escaped and left Jack at our door."

"These are very creative theories," says Lou.

"Does Jack really look like a mad dog to you?"

"He looks exhausted," Dean says. "I hope he's alright. Bobs, is it OK if Jack stays here tonight?"

"Sure," says Bob Four, "it is okay with me."

"Tomorrow," says Lou, "we'll solve this mystery."

Dean gives Jack water and some of Chopper's dog food.
Now Chopper is in a *really* bad mood.
In Dean's room, Jack curls up in Chopper's dog bed.
Chopper sulks and sleeps in the kitchen instead.

CHAPTER 3
DOG SITTING

Lou Tweet makes phone calls late into the night.
She heads for the Bobs' house right at daylight.
She rings the bell; Bob Four answers the door.
"Can't anyone sleep around here anymore?"

Lou runs up the stairs. "Dean! Let's get going.
My Jack Plan ideas have really been flowing.
I called Ms. Pat's friend, the vet, Dr. Tran.
She said to bring Jack in as soon as we can."

"A microchip scan will tell us if he's lost."
"I wonder," says Dean, "how much that will cost."
"Don't worry," says Lou, "the chip scan is free.
Dr. Tran said she'll help us and not charge a fee."

"I briefed Captain Jo'leen on Jack's situation.
We must file a report down at the station.
I called all our friends to meet here around ten.
Brea will bring the new neighbor. Her name is Jen."

"We Bonefish Street kids should be able to find,
The nasty dog haters who left Jack behind.
No way are we going to give this dog back.
We will find a safe home for sweet, little Jack."

Chef Bob makes them breakfast of egg in the hole.
Jack nibbles some kibble from Chopper's food bowl.
Chopper moves far away from this unwelcome pet.
"Stay here," Dean commands. "We're taking Jack to the vet."

CHAPTER 4
CHECKUP

"Jack is healthy and strong!" the vet tells Dean and Lou.

"He seems so weak," says Dean. "What should we do?"

Dr. Tran says, "Try hugs. Have fun and play.

Like you and Chopper do every day."

"We had to leave Chopper at home," explains Dean.

"Since Jack arrived, he's been acting so mean."

Dr. Tran says, "Be patient. It can be hard

When a brand-new dog just shows up in your yard."

At the police station they find Captain Jo'leen.

"Where is Chopper, your buddy?" the captain asks Dean.

Dean hangs his head. Lou explains with a frown,

"Chopper does not like this new dog in town."

Captain Jo'leen says, "Dean, can I mention?
Before Jack, Chopper got all your attention.
Now Jack's in the mix. Chopper is jealous and sad.
Please be patient with him. Don't get so mad."

They file the report, then head back to Dean's house.
Jack lies still in the wagon, quiet as a mouse.
Nine impatient kids are all waiting outside.
But not Chopper. He bolts and runs inside to hide.

Lou cries, "Ramona and Brea, Sal and Samir!
Sherman, Yvette, Chucky P. You're all here."
"At last! We've been waiting forever," whines Zach.
A girl wheels forward, "Nice work! You found Jack!"

CHAPTER 5

JEN

When he hears the girl's voice, Jack leaps like a rocket.
He jumps on her lap, puts his nose in her pocket.
"Who are you? How do you know Jack?" demands Lou.
"Lou and Dean," Brea cries. "Meet Jen. She is new."

"We moved in last week," Jen says "I'm glad to share.
Bonefish Mews is accessible. Great for my chair.
Grandma Fran lived with us, but she wanted more space.
Now she lives at The Shade, a retirement place."

"Pets are not allowed there. They won't let Jack in.
And he can't stay with us. My Mom just had twins."
Dean asks, "Why did your grandma leave Jack with *me*?"
"Yeah," pipes up Zach. "Why the big mystery?"

Jen says, "I hoped there was a dog lover around.
To rescue Jack from having to go to the pound.
We saw Chopper and you, Dean, the day we moved here."
"That kid," Grandma said, "loves his dog, it is clear."

"I thought if I left Jack here, Dean, with you,
you would figure out the right thing to do."

"I did figure it out!" cries Dean. "I'll be right back.
I got carried away with rescuing Jack.
Dr. Tran and the Captain tried to tell me.
To treat Chopper, my buddy, more patiently."

Dean runs in the kitchen. "Chopper, yoo-hoo!
I am so sorry, boy. I was not fair to you."
Dean hugs Chopper tight. "You must never hide.
You are the dog I want right by my side."

CHAPTER 6
MARCH TO THE SHADE

Lou takes the megaphone and starts to shout:

"We had it all wrong. We thought Jack was tossed out.

Let's mobilize! We'll help Jen make her case.

So Grandma Fran can bring Jack to live in her space."

Jen says, "Sign this petition! I'll make us some hats!
The Shade must allow all pets: dogs and cats."
Sherman and Sal yell, "Let's march to The Shade."
"With an escort," Zach adds, "a police motorcade!"

Dean moves through the yard, Chopper right by his side.
Jack sits on Jen's lap as she works, filled with pride.
"I am glad we moved here," says Jen. "It is so neat!
How we all work together on Bonefish Street!"

Ramona makes signs: "Pets Belong in The Shade."
Mayor Mo arrives with Mo's Own Lemonade.
Samir calls Lifeguard Mark. Yvette calls Dr. Tran.
"We need you," they plead. "Come as soon as you can."

Chef Bob packs boxed lunches. Chucky P. maps the route.
Ramona checks the weather. The Tweets pass out fruit.
They get set to go. Chopper and Dean lead the pack,
Then Lou, Pretty Kitty, Mayor Mo, Jen, and Jack.

PETS
belong
THE S

FOR
PETS

THE SHADE
belong in
PETS

"I arranged it," cries Zach. "A police motorcade.
Captain Jo'leen will lead us to The Shade."
Mr. Bigtree starts singing an old protest song.
"Whoop! Whoop!" yell the Bobs, "We are Bonefish Street strong."

CHAPTER 7
MANAGER JOE

They march to The Shade and find Manager Joe.
"Get out of my office. You all have to go.
No pets are allowed here. That is the rule!
Plus, shouldn't you kids all be in school?"

"It's the weekend," states Lou. "There is no school today."
"Manager Joe," cries Dean, "see things our way."
"Jack needs Fran," says Bob Three, as he pats the dog's fur.
"My grandma," Jen says, "needs her dog *here* with her."

Joe scoffs, "No one who lives at The Shade wants a pet.
Pets smell. Make noise. Have to go to the vet.
At The Shade we like things simple and clean.
Where folks live pet-free. Do. You. Get. What. I. Mean?"

"Pets are family," says Dean. "Let people decide—
If they want to live here with their pets by their side."
"Please, Joe," pleads Jen. "Grandma Fran needs her Jack."
"Look! Protests have already started," cries Zach.

CHAPTER 8
PET PROTESTS

"Whoop! Whoop!" Bob Four yells. "Check it out! Look at that. A lovebird. A turtle. A ferret. A cat."

"Grandma," shouts Jen, "and the folks from The Shade!"

"Ooh la la," Sherman cries, "what great costumes they made!"

"Costumes?" grunts Joe. "Shaders, what does this mean?
You are old. You're confused: It is not Halloween."
Jen's Grandma steps forward, "Joe, your words are REFUSED.
We are seniors indeed. But we are NOT confused."

"When I came to The Shade, you did not make it clear
That pets like my Jack are not allowed here."
"Joe, you are the one who's confused," says Bob Four.
"The people have spoken! 'No Pets' is no more!"

Jen wheels to Joe and hands him the petition.
"Bonefish Street folks demand Shade pet admission."
Dean and Lou start the chant: "Say it loud! Say it clear!
Pets of all types are welcome here."

They take turns making speeches. They link arms and sway.
All The Shade residents chant: "Let our pets stay!"
Ms. Pat, her pig, Pippi, and her cat, Donald Crews,
Do an interview with Channel Two News.

Manager Joe stands and packs his briefcase.
"That's it for me. I can't work in this place.
I am scared of all dogs. Birds make me sneeze.
Cats give me horrible skin allergies."

"Find another Shade Manager to work for you!
Good luck to you all. Adios! Ciao. Adieu."

47

CHAPTER 9
VICTORY

"Woo-hoo!" yells the crowd. "We drove Joe away."

"Grandma Fran," cries Jen, "now Jack can stay.

Everyone at The Shade can have pets if they wish."

"I'll hook you up," adds Mark, "if you want some goldfish."

"We won!" Dean agrees. "We all stood our ground.
Now a new Shade Manager needs to be found."
"Dean," whispers Lou, "I know a Bob
Who is perfect to take the Shade Manager job."

"Bob Four," Lou cries, "you have so much to give.
You will run The Shade as a great place to live."
"Great idea," Tweet Four says. "He loves pets, I must say.
Plus, he needs a real job. He just snoozes all day."

Bob Four clears his throat. Wipes a tear, starts to say:
"I will accept this job if we do it my way.
Older folks at The Shade who are living here
Need their Bonefish Street neighbors to all volunteer."

"Tweets will clean," says Tweet Four. "Keep The Shade spick-and-span."

"I'll make house calls each month," says the vet Dr. Tran.

"I'll teach water aerobics on Tuesdays," says Mark.

"And our squad," says Jo'leen, "will patrol after dark."

"Bonefish Glee Club," trills Sherman, "will put on a show."
"I'll be the caller," shouts Zach, "when you play bingo."
"I'll start a book of the month club," Ms. Pat cries.
"We can rock hunt," says Chucky. "It's good exercise."

Bob Four pumps his fist. "Then my answer is YES!
The Shade will be my new office address."
"Bobs and Tweets," Jen cries, " I feel happy and proud!
That our family has joined the Bonefish Street crowd."

CHAPTER 10
BONEFISH STREET STRONG

Later that evening . . .

"Your move," says Lou as she captures Dean's queen.

"Lou, you are a true chess master," groans Dean.

"I practice a lot," Lou smiles. "No one can beat me.
Look! It's five-fifty-five! Quick! Turn on the TV."

Six Tweets and five Bobs, Chopper, and Dean,
Pretty Kitty and Lou, sit around the big screen.
"Jen's grandma!" Dean cries. "Ms. Pat! Donald Crews.
I see Jen and Sherman! We all made the news."

Bob Four comes on-screen. "Whoop! Whoop!" the Bobs cheer.

"I am," Bob Four says, "the new manager here."

The reporter says: "Tell us! Was there a fight?"

"Bonefish kids," Bob Four answers, "stood up for what's right."

The reporter turns next to Jen, Dean, and Lou.

"Bonefish kids?" she asks. "What are your points of view?"

"We organized," Lou says. "Bonefish Street folks stood strong."

"It was unfair," says Jen. "That no-pets rule was wrong."

"This is Chopper," Dean adds, "my pal, loyal and true.
Without him by my side, I don't know what to do.
It was wrong that Jen's Grandma could not live with Jack.
We mobilized to help her get her pet back."

"We are Bonefish Street Strong. We get the job done.
When our community comes together as one.
On Bonefish Street, we will not live apart,
From the people—and pets—who are close to our hearts."

THE END